This book belongs to:

_____

Contributing Illustrators
Karen Craig, David Cutting, Yo-Lynn Hagood, Traci Paige Johnson, Soo Kyung Kim,
Jennifer Oxley, Jenine Pontillo, Tammie Speer-Lyon

With special thanks to illustrators
Michael Lapinski and Khalida Katz Lockheed

Based on the TV series Blue's Clues® *created by Traci Paige Johnson,*
Todd Kessler, and Angela C. Santomero as seen on Nick Jr.®

Simon Spotlight

An imprint of Simon & Schuster Children's Publishing Division
1230 Avenue of the Americas, New York, NY 10020

Book design by Chani Yammer
Manufactured in the United States of America
First Edition
2 4 6 8 10 9 7 5 3 1
Library of Congress Cataloging-in-Publication Data
The Blue's Clues nursery rhyme treasury.— 1st ed.
p. cm.
"Based on the TV series Blue's Clues created by Traci Paige Johnson,
Todd Kessler, and Angela C. Santomero as seen on Nick Jr."—T.p. verso.
ISBN 0-689-84682-7
1. Nursery rhymes. 2. Children's poetry. [1. Nursery rhymes.] I. Blue's Clues (Television program)
PZ8.3 .B59855 2001   398.8—dc21   2001032050

The Blue's Clues Nursery Rhyme Treasury

SIMON SPOTLIGHT/NICK JR.

New York   London   Toronto   Sydney   Singapore

CONTENTS

oink

oink

PAT A CAKE

Pat a cake, pat a cake,
    baker's man,
Bake me a cake as fast as
    you can.
Roll it, and prick it,
And mark it with a "B,"
And put it in the oven
    for Blue and me!

ROUND AND ROUND THE GARDEN

Round and round the garden
Like a teddy bear;
One step, two step,
Tickly under there!

PEASE PORRIDGE HOT

Pease porridge hot,
Pease porridge cold,
Pease porridge in the pot
   nine days old.
Some like it hot,
Some like it cold,
Some like it in the pot
   nine days old.

JACK BE NIMBLE

Jack, be nimble,
Jack, be quick,
Jack, jump over
The candlestick.

RUB-A-DUB-DUB

Rub-a-dub-dub,
Three men in a tub,
And who do you think
    they be?
The butcher, the baker,
    the candlestick maker—
Turn them out,
    knaves all three.

Baa, Baa, Black Sheep

Baa, baa, Black Sheep,
Have you any wool?
Yes, sir, yes, sir,
Three bags full.
One for the master,
And one for the dame,
And one for the little boy
Who lives down the lane.

ONE POTATO, TWO POTATO

One potato, two potato,
Three potato, four,
Five potato, six potato,
Seven potato, more.

OLD MACDONALD HAD A FARM

Old MacDonald had a farm, E-I-E-I-O.

And on his farm he had a cow, E-I-E-I-O.

With a moo, moo here,

And a moo, moo there,

Here a moo,

There a moo,

Everywhere a moo, moo.

Old MacDonald had a farm, E-I-E-I-O.

Old MacDonald had a farm, E-I-E-I-O.
And on his farm he had a pig, E-I-E-I-O.
With an oink, oink here,
And an oink, oink there,
Here an oink,
There an oink,
Everywhere an oink, oink.
Old MacDonald had a farm, E-I-E-I-O.

Old MacDonald had a farm, E-I-E-I-O.
And on his farm he had a horse, E-I-E-I-O.
With a neigh, neigh here,
And a neigh, neigh there,
Here a neigh,
There a neigh,
Everywhere a neigh, neigh.
Old MacDonald had a farm, E-I-E-I-O.

Old MacDonald had a farm, E-I-E-I-O.
And on his farm he had a sheep, E-I-E-I-O.
With a baa, baa here,
And a baa, baa there,
Here a baa,
There a baa,
Everywhere a baa, baa.
Old MacDonald had a farm, E-I-E-I-O.

Old MacDonald had a farm, E-I-E-I-O.
And on his farm he had a duck, E-I-E-I-O.
With a quack, quack here,
And a quack, quack there,
Here a quack,
There a quack,
Everywhere a quack, quack.
Old MacDonald had a farm, E-I-E-I-O.

Old MacDonald had a farm, E-I-E-I-O.
And on his farm he had a frog, E-I-E-I-O.
With a ribbit, ribbit here,
And a ribbit, ribbit there,
Here a ribbit,
There a ribbit,
Everywhere a ribbit, ribbit.
Old MacDonald had a farm, E-I-E-I-O.

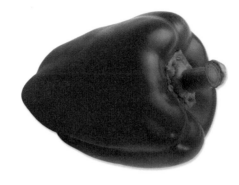

PETER PIPER

Peter Piper picked a peck of
  pickled peppers.
A peck of pickled peppers
  Peter Piper picked.
If Peter Piper picked a peck of
  pickled peppers,
Where's the peck of pickled peppers
  Peter Piper picked?

ROUND AND ROUND AND ROUND

Round and round and round Blue goes,
And where she stops, nobody knows.
Point to the east, point to the west,
Point to the one that you love the best.

LITTLE BLUE HORNER

Little Blue Horner
Sat in a corner
Eating a Christmas pie.
She put in her thumb
And pulled out a plum
And said, "What a good girl am I."

SHOVEL AND PAIL

Shovel and Pail
Went up the hill
To fetch a pail of water.
Shovel fell down
And broke his crown
And Pail came tumbling after.

I Scream

I scream,
You scream,
We all scream,
For ICE CREAM!

She Sells Seashells

She sells seashells
    on the seashore.
The shells that she sells
    are seashells I'm sure.
So if she sells seashells
    on the seashore,
I'm sure that the shells
    are seashore shells.

ARE YOU SLEEPING?

Are you sleeping?
Are you sleeping?
Paprika?
Paprika?
Morning bells are ringing.
Morning bells are ringing.
Ding, dong, ding.
Ding, dong, ding.

HICKORY, TICKETY, TOCK

Hickory, tickety, tock,
The mouse ran up the clock.
The clock struck one,
The mouse did run,
Hickory, tickety, tock.

Rain, Rain, Go Away

Rain, rain, go away.
Come again another day.
Rain, rain, go to Spain.
Never show your face again.
Rain, rain, pour down.
But not a drop on our town.
Rain on the green grass,
And rain on the tree,
And rain on the housetop,
But not on me.

HEY DIDDLE DIDDLE

Hey diddle diddle

The cat and the fiddle,

The cow jumped over the moon.

The little dog laughed

To see such fun,

And the dish ran away with the spoon.

Sippity Sup

Sippity sup, sippity sup,
Bread and milk from a china cup,
Bread and milk
    from a bright silver spoon,
Made of a piece
    of the bright silver moon!
Sippity sup, sippity sup,
Sippity, sippity sup!

LITTLE BLUE PEEP

Little Blue Peep has lost her sheep
And can't tell where to find them.
Leave them alone, and they'll
   come home,
Wagging their tails behind them.

THE ITSY BITSY SPIDER

The itsy bitsy spider
Went up the water spout;
Down came the rain
And washed the spider out.
Out came the sun
And dried up all the rain.
And the itsy bitsy spider
Went up the spout again.

SIX LITTLE DUCKS

Six little ducks that I once knew,
Fat ducks, pretty ducks they were, too.
But the one little duck with the
    feather on his back,
He led the others with his
    quack—quack—quack.
Quack—quack—quack,
    quack—quack—quack.
He led the others with his
    quack—quack—quack.
Down to the meadow they would go,
Wig-wag, wiggle-wag, to and fro.

But the one little duck with the feather
    on his back,
He led the others with his
    quack—quack—quack.
Quack—quack—quack,
    quack—quack—quack.
He led the others with his
    quack—quack—quack.

ROSES ARE RED

Roses are red,
Violets are blue,
Sugar is sweet,
And so are you.

HERE WE GO ROUND THE MULBERRY BUSH

Here we go round the mulberry bush,
The mulberry bush, the mulberry bush.
Here we go round the mulberry bush,
So early in the morning.

These are the things we'll do this week,
Do this week, do this week.
These are the things we'll do this week,
So early every morning.

This is the way we go to school,
Go to school, go to school.
This is the way we go to school,
So early Monday morning.

This is the way we eat our snack,
Eat our snack, eat our snack.
This is the way we eat our snack,
So early Tuesday morning.

This is the way we tie our shoes,
Tie our shoes, tie our shoes.
This is the way we tie our shoes,
So early Wednesday morning.

This is the way we take a bath,
Take a bath, take a bath.
This is the way we take a bath,
So early Thursday morning.

This is the way we brush our teeth,
Brush our teeth, brush our teeth.
This is the way we brush our teeth,
So early Friday morning.

This is the way we read our books,
Read our books, read our books.
This is the way we read our books,
So early Saturday morning.

This is the way we sing our songs,
Sing our songs, sing our songs.
This is the way we sing our songs,
So early Sunday morning.

Here we go round the mulberry bush,
The mulberry bush, the mulberry bush.
Here we go round the mulberry bush,
So early in the morning.

There Was a Little Turtle

There was a little turtle
Who lived in a box.
He swam in the puddles
And climbed on the rocks.
He snapped at the mosquito,
He snapped at the flea,
He snapped at the minnow,
And he snapped at me.
He caught the mosquito,
He caught the flea,
He caught the minnow,
But he didn't catch me!

DOWN AT THE STATION

Down at the station early
in the morning,
See the little puffer bellies
all in a row.
See the engine driver
pull the little throttle;
Puff, puff. Toot! Toot!
Off we go.

LITTLE PUPPY BLUE

Little Puppy Blue
Lost her holiday shoe.
What can Little
    Puppy do?
Give her another to
    match the other,
And then she may
    walk out in two!

To Market, To Market

To market, to market,
    to buy a fat pig.
Home again, home again,
    jiggety jig.
To market, to market,
    to buy a fat hog.
Home again, home again,
    jiggety jog.

PERI, PERI QUITE CONTRARY

Peri, Peri, quite contrary,
How does your garden grow?
With silver bells and cockleshells,
And pretty maids all in a row.

One, Two, Three, Four, Five

One, two, three, four, five,
Once I caught a fish alive.
Six, seven, eight, nine, ten,
Then I let it go again.

Do Your Ears Hang Low?

Do your ears hang low?
Do they wobble to and fro?
Can you tie them in a knot?
Can you tie them in a bow?
Can you throw them o'er your shoulder
Like a continental soldier?
Do your ears hang low?

Do your ears stick out?
Can you waggle them about?
Can you flap them up and down
As you fly around the town?
Can you shut them up for sure
When you hear an awful bore?
Do your ears stick out?

Do your ears stand high?
Do they reach up to the sky?
Do they hang down when they're wet?
Do they stand up when they're dry?
Can you signal to your neighbor
With the minimum of labor?
Do your ears stand high?

MAGENTA HAD A LITTLE LAMB

Magenta had a little lamb.
Its fleece was white as snow.
And everywhere that Magenta went
The lamb was sure to go.
It followed her to school one day.
That was against the rule.
It made the children laugh and play
To see a lamb at school.

Row, Row, Row Your Boat

Row, row, row your boat
Gently down the stream.
Merrily, merrily, merrily, merrily . . .
Life is but a dream.

LITTLE MISS MUFFET

Little Miss Muffet
Sat on a tuffet
To eat her curds and whey.
Out came a spider
And sat down beside her
And frightened Miss Muffet away.

I'm Just as Happy as a Big Sunflower

I'm just as happy as a big sunflower
That nods and bends in the breezes.
My heart's as light
    as the wind that blows,
Blowing from off the trees-es.
I'm just as happy as a butterfly
That dips and spins in the flowers.
My song's as joyous as the pretty birds'
Singing to us for hours.

TWINKLE, TWINKLE, LITTLE STAR

Twinkle, twinkle, Little Star,
How I wonder what you are.
Up above the world so high,
Like a diamond in the sky.
Twinkle, twinkle, Little Star,
How I wonder what you are.

Teddy Bear, Teddy Bear

Teddy Bear, Teddy Bear,
Turn around.
Teddy Bear, Teddy Bear,
Touch the ground.
Teddy Bear, Teddy Bear,
Show your shoe.
Teddy Bear, Teddy Bear,
That will do.
Teddy Bear, Teddy Bear,
Turn out the light.
Teddy Bear, Teddy Bear,
Say good night.